I Want to Be A TEACHER

By Michaela Muntean
Illustrated by David Prebenna

A SESAME STREET/GOLDEN PRESS BOOK
Published by Western Publishing Company, Inc.,
in conjunction with Children's Television Workshop.

I like school. I like my classroom and my desk. I like my teacher, Mr. Redman, too. Someday I am going to be just like him.

To be a good teacher you have to know a lot of things. You have to know the alphabet, and you have to be a good reader. You have to know all about numbers and colors and shapes, and you have to know lots of songs and stories.

Sometimes Ernie and I play school at home. We set up our desks and chalkboard in the living room. We pretend it's a classroom.

One rainy day we decided to play school. I put the chalkboard next to my desk because I was going to pretend to be Mr. Redman. Everything was ready, but Ernie wasn't sitting at his desk. He was in the kitchen.

"What are you doing?" I called to him.

"I'm packing my lunch," Ernie answered.

"Hurry up!" I said. "It's time for school to start."

"Gee, Bert," Ernie said when he finally finished, "where is my cubby for my stuff?"

We didn't have a real cubby, so we decided that Ernie should put his lunch box in the closet.

I said, "Good morning, class," just like Mr. Redman does. "Today we are going to learn about weather."

Ernie raised his hand. "I want to know whether or not it will keep raining all day," he said. "Hee-hee-hee. Do you get it, Bert? *Whether* it will rain…"

"Yes, Ernie, I get it," I said. "Now please pay attention."

So I started to teach. I wrote the word SNOW on the chalkboard. I told Ernie that no two snowflakes are alike. Each one has its own special pattern.

For art time we cut snowflakes out of white paper and hung them up.

"Gee, Bert," said Ernie, "this is fun. And look. No two are alike!"

Then I wrote the word WIND on the chalkboard.
We turned on the fan and pretended it was the wind
blowing our snowflakes.

Next I wrote the word RAIN. We could see what rain was like by looking out the window. So we practiced our numbers by counting the raindrops on the windowpane. We counted twenty-four.

At music time we sang "The Itsy-Bitsy Spider"
because it was the only song I knew that had rain in it.
It goes like this:

The itsy-bitsy spider climbed up the water spout.
Down came the rain and washed the spider out.
Out came the sun and dried up all the rain,
And the itsy-bitsy spider climbed up the spout again.

For story time I read *The Brave Little Pigeon* to Ernie.
It is a story about a pigeon named Puffy. Puffy has to fly
through a terrible snowstorm to deliver an important
message. The message saves everyone in the town, and
Puffy is a hero. It is one of my favorite stories.

After story time, we had quiet time. Ernie got his
blanket and spread it out on the floor. While he rested,
I sharpened pencils and straightened up my desk.

When quiet time was over, I wrote the words SPRING, SUMMER, FALL, and WINTER on the chalkboard. We talked about the different kinds of weather in each season.

I asked Ernie to draw a picture of a tree in each season. He drew one tree with a few little leaves, one tree with lots of green leaves, one tree with red and yellow leaves, and one tree with snow on the branches. It was a good picture. I told Ernie I liked it.

Then I taught Ernie a poem. Uncle Bart taught it to me, and this is how it goes:

Oh, trees, you are so silly.
You wear a lot when it's hot
And nothing when it's chilly!

Ernie liked the poem and said it five times so he wouldn't forget it.

"For alphabet time we are going to play a word game," I said. "What letter does the word WINDOW start with?"

"*W*," said Ernie. "WINDOW starts with the letter *W*. If you look out the WINDOW, Bert, you'll see that it has stopped raining and the sun is shining. Is it time for lunch? We could eat in the park. I packed a sandwich for you, too."

I wanted to go on teaching, but I was hungry, too. So I said, "School is over for today. Let's go outside and enjoy the weather."

Ernie ran to get his lunch box. Then he raised his hand.

"Do you have a question?" I asked. I sounded just like Mr. Redman.

"No, I have something to say," said Ernie.

"What is it, Ernie?" I asked.

"I just want to say that you are really good at teaching, old buddy. I learned a lot today!"

I smiled. "Oh, I am so glad," I said. "Because when I grow up, I want to be a teacher!"